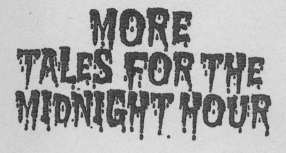

MORE
TALES FOR THE
MIDNIGHT HOUR

MORE TALES FOR THE MIDNIGHT HOUR

13 STORIES OF HORROR

J.B. STAMPER

AN
APPLE
PAPERBACK

SCHOLASTIC INC.
New York Toronto London Auckland Sydney

ISBN 0-590-43998-7

12 11 10 9 8 7 6 5 4 3 2 1   0 1 2 3 4 5/9

Printed in the U.S.A.   01

First Scholastic printing, October 1987

Contents

The Shortcut

People ask me why I've changed. They say I'm too quiet, too withdrawn; some even say I've become a little strange. Well, it's true, I have changed. Ever since that night last summer. . . .

It had been a perfect summer day. I had gone swimming in a pond a few miles from my uncle's farm where I was staying for the month of July. A group of kids who lived in the nearby town were there, too. After swimming, we bought some food and had a picnic in the park. Before I realized how late it was, the sky had started to grow dim with the twilight. The rest of the kids started for home in the town. I was the only one who had to ride the long way to my uncle's house.

I raced my bike hard up the big hill outside town in the direction of the farm. By the time I got to the crest, I had to stop. I was so exhausted that my legs trembled. I stood still on the top of the hill, alone on the road, with my bike leaning against me. I was too tired to go on, too tired to do anything but watch the setting sun. It had sunk so low that it looked like a huge, burning ball in the dark blue sky. Blood-red streaks shot out from it across the horizon.

I shuddered suddenly and felt a chill pass through my body. It seemed I was the only person alive in the world. This part of the country was remote and lonely, and I wasn't familiar with it.

Looking down the hill, I saw where the road split into two forks. I had driven down this hill with my uncle several times. He had taken the road to the right, which was hilly and went past farmhouses. I knew it would be a long, hard ride to get home on that road. When I had asked my uncle about the road to the left, he had said it was the shortcut. Then he had mumbled something about people never taking it. I couldn't remember exactly what he had said.

All around me, the color of the sky deepened to a purplish black. The last red rays of the sunset had faded from the horizon. I knew I had to get back to my uncle's farm as fast as I could. I swung my leg over the bike and pushed off down the hill. When the road split ahead of me, I took the left turn . . . onto the shortcut.

My bike shot down the old dirt road, raising a cloud of dust around me. In the dim light I could see that there were no other tracks on the ground. I started to put on the brakes, suddenly wishing I had taken the more familiar road. Then I realized that I had been steadily coasting downhill. To turn back would mean climbing uphill again. I rode on, down the deserted road.

Finally the ground leveled out, and I had to push hard on the pedals to keep up my speed. My legs ached, but I ignored the pain. I was flying down the road in almost total darkness now. The only light came from a thin moon that hung like a sickle in the black sky.

Then even that light was blotted out by a cloud that moved across the moon. At first I couldn't sense where the road was in front of me. But slowly my eyes, like a cat's, grew used to seeing in the dark. I followed the road that stretched like a ghostly ribbon through the darkness on both sides.

Suddenly the front wheel of my bike hit a hard bump. I struggled to keep it under control, gripping the handlebars so tightly that my hands ached.

The clouds over the moon parted just then. Ahead of me, bathed in eerie moonlight, was an old graveyard. Standing in the middle of the white tombstones was the huge black shadow of a decaying house.

A lump of fear rose in my throat. I started to pump my legs on the pedals as fast as I could. I drew nearer and nearer to the cemetery. But my bike seemed to be going slower and slower. Then, through the panic in my mind, the truth came to me. The front tire of my bike was losing air. Its slow, hissing sound mocked me as I struggled uselessly to pedal forward on the road.

The bike slowed down to a crawl, then it came to a total stop right in front of the graveyard. I looked at the white tombstones, lined up like soldiers in the moonlight. They seemed to stare back at me with curious, sinister eyes hidden in their cold marble.

For a minute I thought about running away, leaving my bike behind. But I forced myself to stoop down and inspect the front wheel. As I had feared, all the air had leaked out.

I heard a noise behind me, a strange rattling noise, coming from the cemetery. I jumped to my feet and cowered against the bike. Again I considered running. But then, all was deadly silent. I reached down and pulled the air pump from the crossbar of my bike.

My hands were shaking, and I dropped the pump against the metal spokes of the back wheel. The noise echoed from one tombstone to another as I bent to pick it up. Still trembling, I found the tire valve and fastened the pump onto it just in time, for then the moon disappeared behind the clouds again, and I was left in total darkness.

I started the pump, afraid to think what I would do if it didn't work. But it did work. The air went in and out, in and out, sounding like heavy breathing. I was breathing hard, too, my breath coming in short gasps. Then, suddenly, I stopped. The sound, the same rattling sound that I had heard before, came from behind me again. The pump hissed louder and louder as I worked it harder. But the rattling grew louder and louder, too. It was coming toward me, closer and closer, through the black night.

I had to escape whatever was making that horrible sound. I pulled the pump off the tire and threw it on the ground by the graveyard. Jumping up, I started to swing my leg over the bike. Then I felt something that made my blood run cold. Five sharp points were stroking the top of my head. They seemed to dig into my brain.

I tried to tell myself that it was the branch of a tree, but the five points began to move down toward my neck. My legs were numbed with fear, but I forced them onto the pedals. Then, with one great lunge of fear, I shot forward on the road.

Whatever had been reaching for my neck was gone now. I had escaped its horrid grip. The bike flew through the darkness, leaving the tombstones to stare at my fleeing back. My body felt as cold as death. Still, my legs worked automatically, pushing the pedals up and down, carrying me away from whatever had touched me in front of the cemetery.

I shot through the darkness, going as fast as I could until my front tire hit another bump. I kept control of the wheels, but a sickening fear spread through my mind. The sound, that horrid rattling sound, was still right behind me!

I pumped harder and harder on the pedals. My breath came in short, painful gasps. I rode on for several minutes, thinking I was safe. Then I heard it again, the rattling. I was afraid to turn around, afraid to see what was chasing me down the dark, lonely road. Time and time again, the rattling sounded behind me. It played on my nerves until I thought I would descend into madness and never return.

Finally, in the moonlight, I caught sight of my uncle's farm. I turned onto the road that led up to his house. He was standing in front, gazing down the road, waiting for me. As soon as I saw him, I tried to tell myself that it had all been my imagination — the staring tombstones, the strange rattling. I rode my bike up to where he stood and jumped off, breathing so desperately that I couldn't speak. I waited for him to say something; but, instead, a look of horror came over his face. He was staring at the seat of my bike.

Trembling, I turned around. There, clamped onto the back of the seat in a grisly death grip, was the rattling, bony hand . . . of a skeleton.

Trick-or-Treat

Martin pressed his face close to the small-paned window in his grandmother's front door. He stared out at the street beyond the overgrown yard. The shadows of night were falling over the late-autumn afternoon. Small children dressed as witches, ghosts, and goblins scurried along the sidewalk. From where he silently watched, Martin could sense their fear. The fun of Halloween was turning to fright as the full moon began to shine in the sky.

Martin's thoughts wandered to his real home. If he were there with his friends, they would begin to trick-or-treat soon. Halloween was always like that. Darkness scared the younger children off the street. Each hour of night brought out the older and braver ones.

This year things were different. Martin's parents had left him with his grandmother while they went on a vacation. Martin hadn't been in this town since he was a young child. He didn't know anyone in it except his grandmother. If he wanted to go trick-or-treating, he would have to go alone.

Martin turned away from the window when he heard his grandmother's footsteps on the staircase.

"Martin, I found it," she said as she walked into the front hallway. "It was just where I thought it would be . . . in that old trunk in the attic."

His grandmother held up a long, black cape for Martin to see. It was made of a heavy, shiny material and had a brass clasp at the neck.

"Your grandfather used to wear this for fancy dress occasions in the city," she said. "But you can wear it tonight . . . if you still want to go trick-or-treating."

A strange tingle of excitement ran through Martin's body. The black cape had an air of mystery and horror. It looked as though it had belonged to Count Dracula. Martin was already dressed in black jeans and a black turtleneck. With the cape on, he could become a creature of the night.

"I'd rather die than miss trick-or-treating," Martin said, taking the cape from his grandmother's outstretched hands.

"Now, Martin," she said, "be careful. I

don't like you roaming around in a town strange to you. It makes me nervous. But your mother insisted I let you go out for Halloween. She said it's your favorite time of the year."

Martin lowered his head so his grandmother wouldn't see the smile that played on his lips. It was true; he did love Halloween. He loved to slip through the dark night like a vampire bat. He loved to scare. . . .

"Don't worry about me, Grandma. I can take care of myself."

Martin took the cape and swirled it around his shoulders. It settled on his body like a smooth skin. He fastened the brass clasp around his neck and folded up the pointed collar around his face. The weight of the cape gave him a sense of power.

Martin looked at his grandmother's anxious face.

"Bye, Grandma. Don't wait up for me."

He slipped out the door before she could say when she wanted him to be home.

"Martin . . . Martin. . . ."

Her worried voice echoed through the night air as he stealthily moved into the shadows of the towering fir trees in the front yard.

From his hiding place Martin looked

back at the old house. His grandmother stood on the porch, peering out into the deepening twilight. Finally she turned, walked back into the house, and shut the door. Martin felt a twinge of guilt along with his relief. She would worry. But at least he hadn't lied to her. She never would have permitted him to stay out as late as he planned to.

Martin felt for the tube of white face paint that he had hidden in his jeans pocket. He pulled it out, put some on his fingertips, and rubbed it across his face. He carefully hid the tube in a crook of the tree branches. From the other pocket he pulled out the fangs he had bought that afternoon from a local store. He fit them into his mouth and then smiled, wishing he could see himself in a mirror.

Two girls dressed as rock stars were coming down the sidewalk past the house. Martin could hear them talking and giggling. Like an animal waits for its prey, he waited until they were in front of the fir trees. Then he sprang out from the shadows.

Their frantic screams pierced the night air as they turned and ran back down the street. Martin wrapped the cape around him and started down the sidewalk in the opposite direction. The night was still young, and already he had felt the thrill of fear. Halloween was even better in this strange town.

Martin slipped from shadow to shadow down the streets, avoiding the patches of light from street lamps. He hid behind bushes when other costumed trick-or-treaters walked by. He waited until he was all alone to walk up to a house and ring the door bell.

"Trick-or-treat."

People didn't like the way he said it. Martin bared his fangs in a smile when they gave him candy. He laughed when they quickly shut their doors and turned the locks. Five times he knocked on doors and frightened the people who answered. He threw away the candy they gave him. Candy wasn't what he liked.

Back on the sidewalk, Martin ran up behind a group of children dressed in costumes. He swirled his cape over their heads, let out a snarl, and burst through them, knocking one over. Martin ran off, their screams of terror echoing after him.

"Hey, you!" a loud, rough voice called out.

Martin looked back and saw a burly man pursuing him down the sidewalk.

"Who do you think you are, scaring my

kids?" the man shouted, his voice heavy with anger.

Martin's feet pounded against the sidewalk. He could hear the man coming up closer and closer behind him. Ahead, off to the right, Martin saw a path going into a stand of trees. He plunged down it just as the man was about to catch him.

The path quickly became narrow and dense with undergrowth. Thorny bushes tore at Martin's face and hands. They forced him to slow down. Martin could still hear the man's panting breath through the silence of the night, but now it was farther away. He pushed on through the thicket of branches. Finally he staggered to a stop and listened. There was no sound in the woods. He turned around. No one was coming after him. Nothing was there. Just the black night.

Martin listened to his breath, coming in short, painful gasps. He became aware of a sharp stinging on his forehead. He touched his finger to the place and felt warm blood. Martin grimaced from the pain, then he smiled. His face must look really horrid now, with the red blood streaked across his white skin.

Martin stared up at the moon and tried to get his bearings in the woods. The trees around him all looked the same. He wasn't

sure which way he had run in from the
street. The path he had followed was lost
somewhere in the dark shadows.

A sharp howl like the cry of a wolf cut
through the air. Martin shivered and drew
the black cape closer around his body.
Suddenly he didn't care anymore about
Halloween night. He only wanted to get out
of these woods and be at home in bed at his
grandmother's.

"The street can't be far," he muttered
to himself.

Martin reached out his arms and began
to push through the underbrush. Without
hesitation he headed in the opposite direction from which the howl seemed to have
come.

Dead twigs snapped under his feet.
Branches with sharp fingers reached out to
tear at his face. Martin walked on through
the woods, losing all sense of time and
direction. The night seemed to close in
around him like a giant black cape cover-
ing the earth. The blackness was not inter-
rupted by the glow of a street lamp or by
the twinkle of a porch light.

Then, suddenly, the clouds parted in the
sky, and the full moon shone down on
Martin's blood-streaked face. He stopped
and looked around him. Had he been going

in circles? Or did these woods go on for miles? Martin slumped against a thick tree trunk in exhaustion. He closed his eyes and fought off the fear that was welling up inside him.

"Are you lost?"

The voice made every nerve in Martin's body jump. He opened his eyes and saw a face only feet away from his. A man was standing there in the pale moonlight, staring at Martin with dark, shining eyes. Martin felt pinned against the tree by his riveting gaze.

No sound came out when Martin opened his mouth to speak. He fought to swallow the lump that lodged in his throat. Finally he stammered out an answer.

"Y-yes, I'm l-lost."

"I'll help you find your way," the man said in a voice that deliberately measured out each word. "I see that you have been trick-or-treating." He paused, staring at the blood on Martin's forehead. "And you've hurt yourself."

"Yes," Martin whispered.

The man finally turned away from Martin and began to walk through the forest in long strides. Martin followed his dark figure in the moonlight, letting a small kernel of hope grow in his mind. Perhaps this stranger would help him out of the woods. Perhaps his nightmare would be over soon.

For a long time there was no sound but the scuffling of leaves under their feet. Martin tried to study the man as he walked behind him. The stranger seemed to be dressed in black, too, although it was difficult to tell in the moonlight. His hair was dark, but his white skin stood out against the night.

"You like to trick-or-treat, don't you, Martin?" the man suddenly asked, not turning around.

"Yes," Martin answered.

Martin laughed nervously. Then his blood ran cold. The man had called him by his name!

"How did you know my name?"

The stranger stopped so quickly that Martin almost stumbled into him.

"Don't be afraid, Martin," the man said. "I know a lot about you. I know how you like Halloween. I know how you like to frighten others."

A strange numbness had come over Martin. He stared into the dark, shining pools of the man's eyes. They seemed to wrap him in a paralyzing trance.

"Come, Martin," the man said. "I will teach you more about fear."

As the man turned around and once again began to walk through the woods, Martin thought about escape. But where would he run to? Surely this stranger could find him even in the darkest hiding place on earth. Martin followed the man like a shadow through the night.

Just when Martin thought he would never again see anything but the dark woods and those black eyes, the stranger suddenly pushed away a branch and stepped onto a paved road. Martin ran out of the woods and stared with relief at a large, old house sitting at the end of a cul-de-sac.

He did not hesitate for a second. Without looking back at the stranger, he took off running toward the house. People would be there, people who would help him when they opened the door.

Martin's heart was pounding as his feet struck the flagstone path that led from the street up to the house. A light was shining above the door, beckoning him to safety. Martin wanted to turn around, to make sure that the man wasn't following him. But he kept on running. All that mattered was that he get to the house.

The door was only feet away. With a desperate lunge Martin grabbed the heavy iron knocker on the door and let it fall against the wood. Then he began to pound his fists on the door, suddenly fearful that no one was inside.

Loud footsteps sounded inside the house. They were coming toward the door. Martin's heart began to beat faster and faster. He heard the doorknob turn. The door swung open with a rusty creak.

Martin was ready to run inside. Then he met the dark, shining eyes of the stranger from the woods. The man stood there, smiling a cruel smile that showed his fangs.

"Trick-or-treat, Martin," the vampire said.

The Hearse

Tim planted his feet in the soft sand and let a cold ocean wave swell up around his ankles. He felt something weird slide across his foot in the water. Looking down, he saw a dead, mangled crab scraping against his leg. He jerked his feet out of the sand and scrambled back on the beach, away from the tide. To his disgust he stepped on another dead crab decaying on the higher shore.

"What's the matter, Timmy? Afraid of the water?"

Tim glanced back at his older sister, Sheila. She was laughing at him behind her big sunglasses. Her skin glistened with tanning lotion in the hot, broiling sun.

Tim walked over to where their parents were sitting under a beach umbrella, reading books. It was their way of spending a summer vacation at the beach.

"Dad, are we going to stay here the

whole week?" Tim asked. "I may die of boredom."

His father slowly looked up from his book. He let out a deep sigh.

"Tim, go for a walk. Try to make friends with other kids on the beach. Collect seashells. Build a sand castle. Anything."

His father stopped talking and went back to his paperback. Tim knew the conversation was over.

"We'll go to the amusement park up the beach tonight, Timmy," his mother said. "You can ride on whatever you want."

"Promise?"

"Promise," she said.

"I'm going for a walk, then. Way down the beach to those dunes you can hardly see from here."

Nobody protested. Tim jogged away, weaving between the groups of sunbathers on the beach. He ran until he reached the last people on the sand, a young couple who wanted to be alone. Once he had passed them, the beach took on a different atmosphere. Tim was all alone, with the crashing waves on one side of him and the hulking sand dunes on the other.

The sun was at its peak in the sky, beating down mercilessly on his face and body. He waded out into the water. The cold, northern ocean felt like ice against his burning skin. He suddenly felt dizzy and ran back onto the blistering sand.

The dizziness didn't go away. Tim knew he needed a drink of water. The heat had dehydrated him. He needed to get out of the direct sunlight for a while at least. He looked around helplessly for some place to hide from its blinding rays.

The soft curves of the sand dunes beckoned him. They looked cooler than the beach. Tim wondered if he could rest there, just until the dizziness passed.

He forced his trembling legs to climb up the first small dune that swelled up from the flat beach. Sea oats grew on its top, but the sand was still scorching hot. Ahead, he saw a larger dune with a sharper crest. Perhaps it would be cooler behind that.

Sand fleas bit at his legs as he stumbled up the big dune. He swatted at the insects, but they were like an army of guerrilla soldiers attacking an invading giant. Tim wiped away the sweat on his forehead and stared at the top of the dune. If he just could get to the other side. . . .

His leaden legs finally reached the top of the dune. He looked down the other side, hoping for shelter from the blistering sun. There was none. The white sand stretched off, unbroken, toward the roadway that ran along the beachfront. Tim looked down the road and was startled to see a lone, black car driving toward him. As it came closer and closer, he realized with a shudder that it was a hearse.

Tim stood on top of the dune, his eyes riveted on the road. The hearse left the road and drove toward him as though he were its destination. It seemed to know that he would be there, waiting for it.

The hearse stopped only feet from where he stood. Tim stared into its darkly tinted windows. Faces veiled with grief and fear stared back at him. Tim rubbed his eyes, wondering if it was a hallucination.

Then the driver's door snapped open. A tall, pale man dressed all in black stepped out onto the sand. He turned his gaunt face up to look at Tim. His eyes were black and bottomless. They focused steadily on Tim's face.

"It's your turn," the driver said in a hollow voice. He gestured to Tim with the long, bony fingers of one hand.

Panic swept over Tim. He looked into the hearse again. A young girl, near his age, sat by the window. She motioned for him to run away. Tim turned from the driver and tried to run up the dune. Then he crumpled into a heap on the sand.

* * *

Slowly his mind swam back to conscious-
ness. Bits of nightmares surfaced and then
submerged again. Finally the itching and
burning of his skin forced him awake.

Tim opened his eyes. The sun was still
burning in the sky. But now it had dropped
lower on the horizon. He sat up and looked
at his skin. It was red and spotted with
swollen bites. The sand fleas had almost
eaten him alive.

He scrambled to his feet and looked
down. Then the memory came back with
a wave of nausea. The black hearse. The
driver's hollow voice. The frightened faces
in the car.

Tim turned and ran down the dune. He
dashed across the wide beach to the ocean.
He ran into the face of a wave, letting it
slap against his body and numb him.

Back on shore again, he whispered to
himself that the memory was from a nightmare. But the driver's eyes still haunted
him. And the words he had said echoed over
and over again in his mind.

He ran back up the beach to where his
family had been. The sand was almost
deserted now. Only a few sunbathers were
left. Tim found where his parents' umbrella had been pulled up. He saw several
wrappers from his sister's favorite chew-

ing gum scattered nearby. They must have gone back to the rented cottage. They were probably angry with him by now for coming back so late and making them worry.

Tim ran harder across the beach, up onto the boardwalk, and over the road. The cottage was two blocks in from the beachfront. Tim wondered if he should tell his parents about the hearse and the driver. They probably wouldn't believe him. And Sheila would make fun of him. He was going to be in enough trouble as it was.

He let the screen door of the cottage slam behind him. His parents came running out from the kitchen.

"We were so worried," his mother said, sobbing.

"I almost called the police," his father added.

Then they both saw his red and swollen body.

Tim let them take care of him. They were so kind that he almost told them about the hearse. But now he didn't want to talk about it. He wanted to forget it, like a horrible nightmare.

To Tim's surprise, his parents still agreed to go to the amusement park that night. The first thing he saw when they drove into the parking lot was the high, wooden framework of the old roller coaster. The first sounds he heard were the screams of the riders as the coaster shot down its steepest drop.

"Those old rides should be torn down," his father muttered as they parked the car.

"I'm going to ride that coaster," Tim said. "You promised I could do whatever I wanted."

"I'm going to ride it, too," Sheila added. "Look, it's called The Tornado."

The Tornado rattled across its tracks high over their heads as they entered the amusement park. Tim's father tried to win a teddy bear by pitching balls at wooden milk bottles. He gave up after missing everything. Sheila stopped to buy some cotton candy. Tim waited impatiently to ride The Tornado.

Finally they walked up in front of the ticket stand for the roller coaster. Tim's father reluctantly paid for two tickets. Tim and Sheila joined a line of eager people nervously laughing as they watched the coaster shoot up and down its curves above them.

"Think we'll get on this time?" Sheila asked as the line dwindled in front of them.

"It'll be close," Tim said.

The coaster screeched to a stop at the

loading platform. The people in the front of the line lunged forward to take the seats that were emptied by the breathless, dazed passengers from the last ride.

Tim watched as the seats quickly filled up. They seemed to be all taken ... but, no, one was left.

A tall, pale man dressed all in black stepped in front of Tim. He was in charge of loading the coaster. He looked at the seats. Then he turned his black, bottomless eyes on Tim.

"It's your turn," the man said in a hollow voice. With the bony fingers of one hand he gestured to Tim to get in the empty seat.

Tim shrank back. He stared at the people's faces in the coaster. A girl's familiar face stared back at him.

The man in black reached out his hand to grab for Tim's arm. Tim backed away, pulling Sheila along with him. They ran past the line of people waiting to buy tickets.

"What are you doing, Timmy?" Sheila gasped.

Tim kept running away from the roller coaster. He didn't look back to see it take off up its treacherous first curve. He didn't look back when he heard the horrible splintering of wood and the wretched screams of the riders. He didn't look back when the crowd began to shout that the old coaster had crashed to the ground.

He ran on and on, trying to escape the man in black ... who was the driver of the hearse.

At Midnight

Isabel stole through the dark shadows of the night toward the clearing in the forest. She wrapped her long cloak around her to keep out the chill of the damp autumn air. There was the sound of a twig snapping behind her. Shuddering, Isabel pressed her body against a thick tree trunk and waited. The forest was quiet. The whole world seemed silent, waiting, like Isabel.

Her mind fled back to the dangerous moments when she had crept out of her father's house. A tall oak tree grew close to her upstairs window. She had climbed onto one of its strong branches and then slipped down from one branch to another, past her father's bedroom window and to the ground. A candle had glowed in the room, casting light on his sleeping face. Then it had sputtered out.

Now Isabel began to run again to the place in the forest where she always met

Thomas. She wanted to arrive first tonight, to watch him ride up on his black horse, the two of them trembling with exhaustion. If all went well, he would be there within the quarter hour. If all went well. . . .

The cold fingers of fear crept around Isabel's mind. She loved a highwayman, a robber who stopped the rich at night in their coaches and stole from them. Thomas only took money from those who had too much; he was a kind and gentle man who never passed a beggar by. But he had a wild nature that showed in his dark eyes. Isabel feared that one night Thomas would meet death instead of her. She also feared her father, who had forbade her ever to see Thomas again.

Isabel pushed aside a low branch and stepped into the clearing. The moonlight shone down through the open space in the canopy of trees overhead. A horse snorted. Isabel's heart jumped, and she whirled around.

Bushes rustled, then a black horse stepped out into the clearing. Thomas's laughter shattered the stillness. He reached down his arms, caught up Isabel, and set her on the horse in front of him.

"I have something to tell you, sweet Isabel," he said. "Tonight was my last night as a highwayman."

Isabel turned to look with wide eyes into his face.

"Tomorrow night," he said, "I'll take you away with me and make you my wife. We'll have a new life, far from your father and far from my past."

When Isabel ran back to her father's house that night, her happiness knew no bounds. The next night, at midnight, she would meet Thomas one last time in the forest. They would run away and be together always.

Thomas rode away happy, too. He weighed in his hand the heavy bag of gold he had stolen that night. It was enough for them to get married, enough to live on for a long time.

When the two young lovers had gone, a dark figure moved from the shadows of an old beech tree at the edge of the clearing. Isabel's father stepped out into the moonlight, his face twisted with hatred and anger.

The next day, the minutes passed like hours for Isabel. She went about her daily chores wearing an air of calmness that hid the turmoil inside her. Her father was especially surly, ordering her to do one thing and then another. By late afternoon, Isabel had gathered together her few precious belongings in a bag that she could easily carry off to the forest that night. She wondered how she could keep up the masquerade of normal life in front of her father until evening.

She did not have to. An hour before suppertime, her Aunt Charlotte rode up to their house in her carriage.

"Isabel, go pack a bag," her father demanded when her aunt came into the house. "You are going home with your aunt. She will keep you for several days."

"But, Father — " she began.

Then she met his eyes and saw the steely, hard look in them. Somehow, he knew.

Hot blood flushed her face; she ran to her bedroom. Quickly she gathered together her bag and another satchel of clothes. She would go with her aunt. But then she would escape and run to the forest, even though it was farther from her aunt's house than her own. She would still meet Thomas, as she had promised, at midnight.

"Hurry now," her father told them as they stepped into the carriage. "Night will fall soon. And the highwaymen will foul the countryside with their thievery."

Isabel avoided her father's face as the carriage jolted forward and then sped away from his house. Her aunt leaned close to her.

"If you try to run away, Isabel," she said, "I will call the sheriff. Your father has told me what to say."

Isabel squeezed her eyes shut to keep the tears from welling up. Her father had thought of everything. If she tried to escape, he would send the sheriff after her. And if the sheriff found Thomas . . .

All through dinner and the long evening at her aunt's house, Isabel kept her composure. But her mind was frantic, devising and then casting away and then revising plans for escape. Finally, at ten o'clock, her aunt led her to a bedroom.

"Go to sleep, Isabel," she said in a firm voice. "But do not try to escape. I will be sitting outside the door."

Isabel gently kissed her aunt on the cheek but did not meet her eyes. She shut the heavy door to the room and latched it. First she went to the windows. She tried to push up on the sashes. Then she saw how strong her prison was. New nails had been pounded into the frames and the sill. She would never be able to open them. And even if she could shatter the glass without her aunt hearing, the panes were too small for her to climb through. Isabel fell onto the bed and wept. Thomas would be waiting for her in two hours.

Isabel woke with a start. Frantically she

looked around the room for a clock. She had cried herself asleep. Now it was midnight. The horrible dream came back. She had been dreaming about Thomas. He had called to her, a terrible scream that had awakened her.

Isabel crept from the bed and slowly opened the door. A chair was sitting in the hallway, but her aunt had left. She threw her cloak around her, tied a warm woolen scarf around her neck, and picked up her bag of belongings. Thomas would still be waiting for her; she was sure.

A short time later Isabel was running through the night toward the clearing in the woods.

Her face was streaked with tears and scratches by the time she reached the clearing. She had run wildly for almost an hour, her heart full of foreboding and fear. Isabel couldn't forget the dream she had had. And Thomas's scream echoed in her mind.

The moonlight shone down on the clearing through a cloudless sky. Isabel searched the shadows. No one was there. Thomas had left her.

Then there was a rustling in the undergrowth of the forest. A black horse rode across the clearing to Isabel. Thomas sat in the saddle, his face a ghostly white in the moonlight.

"Thomas," Isabel called out, and ran to him.

She reached up her arms to him. When he lifted her into the saddle, his hands were icy cold. She shrank away from him, suddenly afraid.

"Thomas," she whispered, "I'm sorry I'm late. It was Father. He tried to keep me away from you. I had to escape from my aunt's house."

"You still came, Isabel," Thomas murmured, his voice weak and low.

"Where shall we go?" she asked, wondering at the change in him. She looked up into his eyes, which were like dark coals in his white face.

"I will take you to where you are safe, Isabel," he said. "Be silent and lean against me. It is so cold."

Isabel pulled off her soft woolen scarf.

"Wear this, Thomas," she said, and lovingly wrapped it around his neck.

Thomas kissed Isabel on the top of her head; they rode in silence through the dark woods.

Isabel shut her eyes and leaned her head into her lover's chest. She could feel the warmth of her body slowly work its way into his heart.

Suddenly the horse stopped. Isabel opened her eyes and saw her aunt's house in front of them.

She looked at Thomas in confusion.

"Good-bye, Isabel," he said, helping her slip to the ground. "Good-bye, my love." Then he leaned down to kiss her.

Isabel shuddered when she felt his cold lips upon hers. She touched his cheek with her hand, staring into his deep eyes. She cried when he rode away into the blackness of the night.

Isabel awoke from a nightmare the next morning. It was Thomas's scream again, calling her name. Her aunt walked into the bedroom, carrying a breakfast tray.

"What is it, child?" she asked.

"Thomas," Isabel whispered. "Why did he leave me last night?"

"Then you know . . ." her aunt said with downcast eyes.

"Know?" Isabel said. Fear welled up in her chest.

"Thomas was hanged by the sheriff at midnight," her aunt said. "He will be buried this morning."

"No!" Isabel gasped. "It isn't true. I met him last night in the forest. It was after midnight. But he had waited. He brought me back here on his horse."

"No, Isabel. That was a dream. Thomas was dead at midnight."

Isabel jumped from the bed and hurriedly dressed.

"Why do you say he is dead? If he is dead, where is his body?"

"In the church crypt," her aunt answered. "But you mustn't go."

Isabel ran from the room and out the door of the house. The church was not far; she ran until her breath tore at her chest. The priest was standing at the doors of the church.

"Thomas!" she cried out to the priest. "It can't be true."

The priest's eyes were full of pity. Isabel rushed past him and down the stairs to the crypt of the church. There, lying in a wood coffin, was Thomas.

Isabel walked slowly toward him. His face was ghostly white, as it had been the night before. His dark eyes were closed forever. And around his neck was the soft, woolen scarf she had put there, to keep her love warm.

The Black Mare

The road wound through the moonlit countryside like a black ribbon, edged on both sides by tall woods except where fields had been cleared and small houses built. This night, two riders galloped down the road, pushing their horses on in a race. Luke Paxton watched his older brother, Michael, pull farther and farther out in front of him. His new mount was no match for Michael's gray stallion, which he had trained and ridden since it was a colt.

They were fools to be racing in the moonlight, but both brothers knew the road well. It led to their father's house, which sat on top of the next ridge. Luke could see his brother's back disappearing into the dark hollow ahead, where the road dipped down into thick, overhanging trees.

Suddenly the night air vibrated with the shrill whinny of a horse. Then a shriek of horror followed, coming from the dark hollow. Luke fought to keep his horse under control. It was suddenly dancing about as though it had been spooked. The hollow was pitch-black; Luke waited for Michael to ride out and up the moonlit road beyond it. But a horrible silence had fallen over the countryside. There was no sound of galloping hooves; there was no sound at all. Luke felt fear creeping through his body like a warm poison. What had happened in the dark hollow? Where was Michael?

He kicked his horse forward, but it reared back, refusing to go. Luke was not a cruel horseman, but now he dug his boots into the horse's side and forced it down the road toward the hollow. Just as they entered its dark shadows, Michael's horse tore past them, a blur of gray without a rider. It galloped up the hill they had just come down, snorting and out of control.

Luke held the reins of his horse tight and rode on. Ahead, he saw a dark figure slumped on the road. Before he reached it, there was another shrill whinny from the forest. Luke looked toward it and saw the flank of a black horse shine in the moonlight, and then disappear.

He dismounted and fell to the ground beside the figure. Turning the body over, he saw his brother's face, contorted in a grimace of death. Michael's chest was crushed, trampled down. Luke lifted his brother's dead body onto his horse and carried it home.

Michael Paxton was the first. Two weeks later another man was found trampled to death, on a different secluded road in the valley. The next week, a carriage traveling at night overturned and killed a young girl. The people with her told of a black mare that tried to attack them but was driven off by the shot of a gun. Fear and superstition spread through the area like wildfire. There was talk of witches for the first time in years.

"You mustn't go out at night," Luke's sister, Emma, pleaded with him. "That horse is possessed by a demon or worse. It's killed three people now."

Luke sat in their house by the fireplace, staring into the leaping flames. He could not forget his brother's death. He wanted revenge on whatever had killed Michael in that brutal way.

"They say it might be a witch," Emma whispered, "a witch in the form of a black mare. There are old stories about such things."

Luke knew the stories. Not so many years ago there had been witch-hunts in the area. Women had been accused of being shapeshifters. He had not believed the stories before, but now he was not so sure.

"I'll get that mare, if it means my death," he murmured under his breath.

Luke began to read books on witchcraft. They were full of superstitions, potions, spells, and charms. He learned about the shapes that witches were said to take . . . how they flew about at night as owls, or prowled around as cats, or galloped about as horses. He memorized chants, practiced making potions, and daily grew more bent on revenge.

One day he went to the blacksmith and asked the smithy to make him four horseshoes for a mare, a large mare. The blacksmith did as he asked and gave Luke the nails he would need to pound the shoes into the hooves of a horse.

Luke took the horseshoes and hung them on a hook in the barn. Then he went back to the witchcraft books. Next he fashioned a rope out of leather strips, braided and knotted in a special way. He hung the rope in the barn beside the horseshoes.

His sister awoke one night and came downstairs to find Luke cooking something over the hearth. He would not show her what was in the pot that he hid from her sight; he quickly slipped a thin book he had been reading inside his jacket.

Finally, one night, all was ready.

Luke crept out of his father's house after the family had gone to sleep. He looked up into the sky at the full moon. It had been a month since Michael was killed in the hollow. Luke went to the barn and gathered the things he needed. Inside his coat pocket he put the small canteen full of the vile liquid he had concocted. He slipped the leather rope over his shoulder. He left the horseshoes where they were on the hook in the barn. Noiselessly he mounted his horse and guided it out of the barn onto the road that led down into the hollow.

The horse was skittish as he nudged it into a canter. He quickly pushed it to a gallop, knowing that if he hesitated, both the horse and he might turn back. They flew down the dark road into the shadows where Michael had died. Luke kept his brother's face in his mind as he pulled his horse to a halt, dismounted, and then slapped its rump to send it away. The horse galloped off back to the barn, leaving Luke alone on the road.

This was the place. Luke stared down at the ground where he had found his brother's body. Then he looked up at the low-hanging branch that crossed the road above the spot. He was suddenly seized by a terror that made him run for the tree and scramble into its branches. The feeling of dread grew and grew as he inched out onto the limb hanging over the road. He knew he had made it with only seconds to spare. The eerie sound of hoofbeats came pounding through the forest.

Luke saw a black shadow flash through the trees and come toward the road. The horse was so close now that he heard its raspy breathing and saw its red eyes glowing in the night. He shrank against the limb, suddenly losing his courage. If the mare saw him there, what could she do? Could she jump into the sky and pull him down to the ground?

Luke tried to remember through his fear what the books had taught him. He pulled the canteen of potion from his coat. With trembling fingers he loosened the stop and tipped the bottle down to the ground. A noiseless stream of liquid fell on the spot where his brother had died. The smell of the potion permeated the night air. The mare snorted as it reached her nostrils.

It happened just as the books on witchcraft said it would. The mare was drawn to the potion as if by magic. It slowly clopped along the road, pulled to the place where the potion lay. Luke braced his body against the limb and readied the rope he had made, with its secret braids and knots.

The mare stopped underneath him, sniffing and lapping at the strange potion. Luke held his breath and dropped the noose of the rope over her head. For a second the red eyes flared up at him and the powerful body reared. But then a trance came over the mare, and Luke knew his spell had worked.

He slipped down from the limb and jumped onto the mare's back, holding on to the end of the rope like a rein. The black mare obeyed his command to gallop; he turned it up the road toward his father's farm. Luke shuddered at the feel of the mare beneath his body. He knew he was riding a witch who had taken the form of a horse and killed with her evil powers.

Luke guided the mare into the open barn door, slipped off her back, and tied the leather rope to a stable post. A cold sweat had come over him now; he knew he must work fast.

He pulled the first horseshoe off the wall, lifted the mare's left foreleg, and pounded the shoe onto the hoof. Quickly he went on to the right foreleg. The mare began to get skittish. Luke looked at her face and thought he saw a red glint flaring up in her eyes. He reached for the third horseshoe and desperately began to pound it into her left hind hoof. As he finished, the mare reared and turned toward him. There was froth at her mouth; her red eyes glowed. The rope pulled loose from the post and the mare shook it off her head. Luke fell back, clutching the fourth horseshoe in his hand. The mare reared again, her front hooves close to his face. Then she galloped from the barn, the spell broken.

Luke waited till dawn crept into the sky. Then he began to track the mare. The prints of the three horseshoes traveled down the road from the barn and into the hollow. Luke followed them as they turned into the woods and crossed over a stream. The tracks were unmistakable to follow. Luke guided his horse after them up a hill and along a ridge.

He was out of the woods now and traveling through some of the best farmland in the area. Ahead he saw the house of the rich widow, Sarah Harding. The tracks of the mare were headed straight for her farm. Luke's mind grew anxious as he thought about the black-haired widow who was still young and beautiful. What if the mare-witch had killed her as it had killed his brother? He kicked the sides of his horse into a gallop.

The mare's tracks ran through the widow's yard. Luke quickly dismounted and hurried to the front door of the Harding house. When he reached it, he heard terrible moans from inside. Luke tried the handle; it wasn't locked. He pushed open the door and rushed inside.

The Widow Harding was sitting by the fireplace, her long black hair hanging disheveled about her face. Luke walked toward her, then stopped. She was staring at him with wild eyes that glinted red in the center. And on her two hands and one foot, Luke saw the three horseshoes he had pounded into the mare's hooves.

The Love Charm

The path to the witch's cottage twisted through high bushes and overhanging trees. More than once, Kate looked behind her. Was it the sound of someone following that she heard? Or was it just the whispering of the trees in the night air? She clutched the money tighter in her hand and hurried on.

A black shadow jumped out onto the path in front of her, making a soft thud when it landed. Kate drew back. Then she saw the green slit eyes of the cat peering at her through the black night. The cat made a strange meow, turned, and walked down the path in front of her, switching its tail back and forth. Kate followed its shadow, for she knew it would lead her to the witch.

Bramble bushes reached out onto the path, pulling at her hair and clothes. Kate pushed them aside, trying to keep up with the cat as it stole its way through the darkness. The path made a sharp turn, and the cat suddenly bounded forward. Then Kate saw it, too. The witch's cottage crouched among the trees as though it were a part of the forest. Only one window had light, the leaping, flickering light of a fire. All else was dark except where the moonlight filtered down through the opening in the forest and shone on the doorway.

Kate moved into the shadow of a huge tree near the end of the path and leaned against its scaly trunk. A thick, sweet aroma of herbs and flowers permeated the air. It overwhelmed Kate with its magical incense. She felt faint.

The cat jumped onto the doorstep and began scratching the wooden door with its claws, all the while making its weird, plaintive cry. Kate hovered in the shadows, watching. The door opened, and the old woman whom the villagers called a witch reached down and picked up her cat. As she stroked its sleek fur she mumbled words to it that Kate couldn't understand. The cat answered with a high whine. Then the witch set it down on the ground and took a step toward the woods.

"Who is there?" she asked in an old, cracked voice.

Kate thought about running away. But she struggled forward from the shadows to face the woman. "I am Kate Allen, a servant in the manor house. A friend told me you make love charms. I want one."

As Kate stepped closer to the witch she could see her long, yellow teeth set in a smile.

"It's a love charm that you want, is it?"

Kate nodded her head.

"Have you got the money for it?" the witch asked. "Love can't be bought cheaply, you know."

Kate opened her hand, in which she had been clutching her last month's wages. "I have this," she said.

The old woman reached out for the coins and picked them from Kate's palm. Then she cackled a satisfied laugh and motioned Kate toward the cottage. Kate followed her into a low-ceilinged room, the room that was lit by the fireplace. Along the walls were shelves and nooks, filled with bottles and jars of every shape and size.

Kate sat down on the low wooden bench by the fire and stared at the old woman as she began to gather a collection of bottles on the table under the shelves.

"I can make what you want, dearie," the witch said, looking at Kate's plain face, lit by the firelight. But it is worth much more than you have given me. Are you sure you don't have more?"

Kate nodded her head solemnly. The old woman cackled again.

"Now you must turn away and look into the fire. If you watch me, the charm will be ruined."

Obediently Kate turned toward the fire and stared into the flames. They made her mind leap and burn. She thought of all the young men she had secretly loved, the young men who had ignored her and married others. She let her mind drift to the dreams that came so often into her head. . . .

"The charm is ready," the old woman said from behind her. "You have lost yourself in the flames."

Kate turned around. In her hands the witch held a small, blue glass bottle. Kate reached out for it, but the witch drew it away.

"No, not yet. Before you touch it, there is something you must know. Whoever drinks this love potion will fall helplessly in love with you. His love will be charmed and will last forever. But. . . ." The witch's eyes narrowed into slits like her cat's. "But if this bottle is ever broken, then the charm will be broken, too."

Again Kate reached out for the precious bottle. The witch gently placed it in her hand. Kate felt the glass burning in her palm with a strange heat, but she held it tightly in her fist.

"There is one more thing," the witch said as Kate rose to go. "Put the bottle under your pillow tonight and you will dream of a man. Give that man this potion, and he will become your husband."

Kate walked out of the cottage and into the darkness of the night. She felt entranced by the witch's words and by the smell of the herbs and flowers. When she opened her hand to gaze at the tiny bottle, the moonlight shone on it, looking as though the moon itself were trapped inside. She closed her fingers tightly around the charm and hurried along the path, back to the manor house where she lived.

The next morning, Kate woke with a start from strange dreams. She looked around her small, plain servant's bedroom. In her dreams she had been the lady of the house; there had been satin sheets on her bed and lace curtains on her windows. . . . Suddenly Kate remembered the love charm. She felt for it under her pillow and pulled it out. The charm had been there all night.

A wave of anger washed over her. The witch had lied when she said Kate would dream of her future husband. Kate had dreamed of her master . . . her master who was rich and handsome and married.

Kate threw the blue glass bottle onto her bed stand. It slid across the top and stopped just near the edge. As she dressed, she decided she would take it back to the witch that night. She wouldn't be cheated out of her money so easily.

When she climbed down the stairs to the kitchen, Kate tried to erase the anger and the dreams from her mind. She busied herself with her morning chores. Then Elsie, the cook, burst through the door that adjoined the main part of the house. She was shaking and sobbing, and her face was swollen red from crying.

"What is it, Elsie?" Kate asked.

"It's too horrible, too horrible," Elsie sobbed.

"What is?"

"It's the master's wife, Katie. She's dead. She died in her sleep last night."

Kate left Elsie sobbing alone in the kitchen. She flew back up the stairs to her room, her mind crowded with horrible and wonderful thoughts that fought each other like good and evil. The glass bottle still rested on the bed stand where she had thrown it. Kate reached for it and held it up in the pale morning light. She gazed into its deep blue color, trying to make sense of what was happening. Before she went back downstairs, she wrapped the bottle in her thickest wool shawl and hid it in the farthest corner of her closet.

Two months passed. Kate quivered inside now when she saw her master. His mourning for his wife had made him thin and pale and less handsome. But as every day went by, Kate fell more and more in love with him. Now she knew it could happen, what the witch had promised.

Every evening, after dinner, Kate brought him his glass of brandy. One night, as usual, he was sitting in front of the fire in his study, sunk deep in melancholy over his wife's death. Kate came into the room with the brandy. She stopped at the bookcase behind him and set the glass on the shelf. Then she felt for the small bottle, hidden deep in the pocket of her dress. Kate pulled it out and for a long while stared at it. Then she poured the sweet-smelling potion into the glass.

With shaking hands she took it to him. Automatically he reached out for his brandy. As he began to sip the drink, Kate ran from the room and stood by the high window in the hall, staring out into the black, mysterious night.

"Kate."

It was his voice, calling her. She trembled in the darkness of the hall. Then she walked into the room and over to the fireplace where he still sat in his chair, the empty glass beside it on the floor. Kate looked into his burning eyes and saw that the love charm had worked.

It was confusing at first, just as the dreams had been. It didn't seem to matter to him that she was a servant and poor and plain. He fell completely in love with her. And the death of his first wife was forgotten; it was almost as though she had never existed.

Of course, people were shocked. Kate was embarrassed by their gossip. Some even whispered that she was a witch. But on the day of their marriage she knew that she had no reason to worry anymore. She was his wife, just as the witch had predicted. And Kate was sure that he would love her forever, for she had hidden the bottle well.

They had been married for a year. Kate, hardly remembering the servant she once was, looked at herself in the gilt-edged mirror of her dressing table. Her face was still plain. But the rich jewels and fine clothes that she wore made her look almost handsome. Her husband told her that she was beautiful.

Kate smiled to herself, suddenly remembering the love charm. She was filled with an overwhelming curiosity to see it again. She had hidden it safely away on her wedding day in a carved wooden box that had been a gift from her husband. Kate wore the key to the box around her neck.

Now Kate wanted to hold the tiny bottle in her hands again. She wanted to look into its deep blue color. She wanted to remember the magic she had felt when the witch first gave it to her.

The carved box was in her closet, hidden under her old, woolen shawl. Kate uncovered it and took off the key from around her neck. Her fingers fumbled nervously as she fit the key into the lock. A thought had crept into her mind and was growing there like a poisonous weed. What if the love charm was no longer in the box? She threw open the lid and reached inside for the bundle of wool that she had wound around the bottle. She unwrapped the wool, layer after layer, until she came to a soft leather bag. She tugged nervously at the drawstring and then felt inside. Her fingers closed around the smooth glass bottle.

A calmness spread through Kate's body. It was safe, the charm and her love. She took the bottle over to the window and held it up to the sun. It caught the sunlight just as it had trapped the moonlight that first night in the witch's garden. Kate turned the bottle around and around, enchanted by its power.

"I love you," her husband whispered in her ear.

Kate jumped in fright. The blue bottle slipped from her hands and fell to the floor at her feet, shattering into a thousand tiny pieces of glass that flew apart in the sunlight. Kate stared at the pieces in horror. Then she slowly turned around to look at her husband.

The witch had been right. At first he gazed at her in confusion. Then his face took on a look of disgust. Soon hatred shone from his eyes that had once burned with love.

"What are you doing here?" he screamed. "Where is my wife?"

Then he fled from her. Kate stood by the window, her body shaking with sobs. She saw him cross the yard below and climb the hill to where his first wife was buried. Kate turned from the window. Her eyes were caught by the twinkling bits of blue glass. They were winking up at her from the floor like laughing eyes.

The path to the witch's cottage was overgrown with tall weeds and sharp thistles. Kate didn't feel the tears in her flesh or see the insects that swarmed around her swollen face. She pushed through the darkness that was falling as black as the doom around her heart.

Suddenly, in front of her, the cat jumped out onto the path. Now Kate sobbed in relief when she saw it. But the cat's green, slit eyes seemed to mock her. It meowed its high, unnatural call and ran off down the path. Kate tried to catch up with it, but the brambles and branches caught at the ribbons on her fine gown and pulled her back like jealous arms.

Finally she smelled the sweet aroma of the herbs and flowers. She knew she was near the witch's cottage. Kate came out of the shadows of the forest and into the opening and saw the witch, standing on her doorstep and petting the cat in her arms. The perfume in the air was potent. The witch was smiling.

"The charm has been broken, I see," she said.

Kate walked up to the witch, her eyes pleading.

"You must help me."

The witch stared off into the black forest. The cat meowed.

"You have broken the glass bottle, and you have broken my charm. Neither can be mended. Now he will hate you as strongly as he once loved you."

The old woman looked down at her cat and stroked its sleek black fur. Then she turned her wise, green eyes on Kate.

"Charmed love is not true love," she said.

The trees whispered it again in Kate's ears. She turned away from the witch's cottage and the sweet perfume of the garden. And she walked away . . . into the black, black night.

The Mask

It was his last night in Africa. Daniel Clarke walked through an open-air market, watching the merchants pack up their wares in the deepening twilight. He was beginning to feel desperate. Although he had found gifts to take back to his wife and son, he hadn't yet found the thing he wanted for himself. It had to be something exotic and mysterious, like Africa was to him.

A beggar reached out and touched his leg, pleading for money. As Daniel dropped a coin in the man's lap, he felt a chill travel through his body. The night was growing cold. He walked on through the darkened streets, moving deeper and deeper into the native quarters of the city, far from the tourist hotels and shops.

He chanced upon a narrow, dark alley that ran off one of the main streets. Daniel knew it was foolish for a stranger, a foreigner, to walk down that road. But there was an open doorway at the end, with light spilling out onto the alley. Daniel felt a premonition that this place held the thing he was seeking.

He started down the narrow, cobble-stoned street, walking in the middle, avoiding the shadows along the sides. Halfway down, he heard breathing from a darkened doorway. He kept walking, hurrying, toward the light.

At the end he panicked and began to run. He burst through the open doorway into a room that glowed with the fires of many small oil lamps. A man with a dark, impassive face and shining eyes stood behind a counter, staring at him.

"The shop is closing," the man said in English in a deep voice.

Daniel's eyes quickly darted around the room. Drums, spears, masks, and other tribal items hung on the walls and sat on the shelves.

"I must close," the man repeated. "My child is ill upstairs."

Daniel could not move from the spot where he stood, gazing at one thing after another. They were what he had been looking for.

"Please," he asked, "I won't take long."

The man stiffened as the cry of a child echoed down from the room above.

Daniel's eyes came to rest on a mask hanging high on the wall near the back of the shop. It was carved of a dark wood, almost black, and had a fringe of real hair, matted and copper-colored, around it.

"That mask. How much is it?"

"Not for sale," the man muttered. "An evil mask, not for tourists."

"No, you don't understand," Daniel protested. "I'm not really a tourist. I'm a writer. I came to Africa to research a book. I want that mask."

The man shook his head firmly from side to side.

"The mask has evil. No one can put it on his face except a man of power — a witch doctor, as you call him. Look for something else."

A wail came from upstairs, and a child's voice called out in an African language. The shopkeeper's eyes grew worried. He looked from Daniel to the stairs and then back to Daniel again.

"Stay," he said. "I must visit my child."

Daniel did not take his eyes off the mask as the man climbed the narrow steps up to the second floor. He drew closer and closer and soon stood just underneath it. He reached up and took the mask in his hands.

Daniel lifted it off the wall. He brought it down and looked at the strange face carved into the wood. The mask willed him to take it. Daniel pulled out a large roll of local currency from his wallet and put the money on the counter. Then he ran back through the doorway into the dark alley and the black night.

Coming back to New York was a shock for Daniel. His time in Africa had made him forget its fast, nervous pace. He felt like a foreigner as he sat in the taxi from the airport, staring at the skyscrapers and the snarl of cars trapped around him.

His wife and son said he had changed. He was tanned and thinner and seemed remote. Daniel felt like a stranger in his own house. He went through the motions of unpacking and giving out the gifts he had brought back. Finally he pulled the mask out of the largest suitcase where he had carefully bundled it between his clothes.

"Weird," his son Mark said when he saw the mask. "Did you buy this from a witch doctor?"

"No, from a shop," Daniel answered, feeling a rush of shame.

Mark picked it up and looked at the face. The mouth was twisted in a mocking smile. The hollow eyes seemed to hide an evil secret. The face was carved with scars. He began to lift it to his face.

"No!" Daniel shouted, remembering the shopkeeper's words. He grabbed the mask from his son's hands.

"Dad, what's the matter?" Mark asked, looking at his father in amazement. "I didn't do anything wrong."

Daniel noticed that his wife was staring at him, too.

"The mask is special," he quickly explained. "No one can put it on his face except a man of power, a witch doctor." Daniel looked down at the mask. His hands were trembling as he held it.

"Come on, Dad, you don't believe in that stuff, do you?" Mark asked.

"Daniel, are you all right?" his wife asked. "Did you catch one of those strange tropical diseases over there?"

"I'm fine!" Daniel snapped. He carefully put the mask back in his suitcase. "I might have a little jet lag, that's all."

The next day Daniel hung the mask on a wall of his study. It was the wall behind which his desk sat overlooking a garden of trees and shrubs. Daniel was happy to get back to work on the book. He sat down at his desk and began writing a long description of the African plains that opened one of his chapters.

Two hours later he pushed his chair

away from the desk. He had finished the chapter. Daniel was sure it was the best writing he had ever done. But suddenly his head had begun to pound with a headache. The pounding was almost like drums, African drums. He turned around.

The mask was watching him, its hollow eyes staring into his face. Daniel felt that they could see through him and read his thoughts. He got up and stepped closer to it. The pounding grew louder and louder. He had the sudden urge to take the mask off the wall. It seemed to be telling him to put it on his. . . .

Daniel ran from the room. He hurried past a mirror in the living room and caught a glance of his face. It was contorted with fear.

The next day Daniel sat down to work at his desk early in the morning. Everyone else in the house was still asleep. He began a new chapter about the jeep ride he had taken across the African plains. He described the giraffe and antelope, the African people and their homes. His pen suddenly stopped moving across the paper. The pounding in his head had started again. The pen dropped from his hand.

Daniel whirled around to face the mask. The weird, matted hair around it seemed to move and then stop. The hollow eyes stared at him.

Daniel was drawn to it. The strange mouth was smiling, telling him to touch it. Daniel reached up and pulled the mask off the wall. It was warm in his hands. He lifted the mask up to his eyes and saw the darkness inside. Then he covered his face with it. The drums were pounding even louder now. Daniel's heart pounded to their rhythm.

"Daniel," a voice said.

He turned to the door. It was his wife.

"Daniel, take off that mask."

Slowly he pulled the mask away from his face. His wife screamed and backed away from him. He stepped toward her, but she ran. He followed her into the living room, glancing at the mirror as he passed by.

A strange man looked back at him. His lips were twisted in a mocking smile. His face was ridged with deep scars. His head was ringed by matted, copper-colored hair.

Daniel dropped his eyes down to the mask in his hands. Staring back at him was a face, the face of the man he had once been.

Right Inn

Philip Mason was a nervous, meticulous man. He planned out each day of his life with such care that he could predict what would happen before it happened. He wore a certain color tie on the same day of each week. He had the same breakfast at exactly seven-fifteen every morning. He was not married, of course. That would mean a wife and probably children; things could get very unpredictable then.

Philip was a traveling salesman, selling his own book, titled *How To Organize Your Life*, to small bookstores. He made a decent living. But he found it rather unsettling to spend nights in different hotel rooms. It was hard to know what to expect. Philip solved the problem by always staying at the Like-Home Hotel chain, where he could count on the same bar of green soap and the same white towels and the same picture of a bullfighter on the wall. He had organized his life very well.

One day Philip found himself taking an unexpected risk. He was in Maine, a state he didn't know well. He had heard of a bookstore in a small town north of the capital that had a large mail-order business. It sounded like a good market, despite its remote location. By late afternoon Philip had found the store, given his sales talk, and sold one hundred of his books.

He stopped by a café to have a cup of coffee and celebrate. While sitting in a cozy booth and looking out at the snow beginning to fall, Philip heard the weather report blare out over the radio. It predicted a heavy winter storm that evening and issued a traveler's advisory. A feeling of panic rose in Philip's chest. This all sounded very unpredictable. He decided to get back to the capital, where there was a Like-Home Hotel, as soon as possible.

As he warmed up his car's motor, Philip checked the Maine road map that he had purchased as soon as he'd crossed the state line. The best route back to the capital seemed to be a two-lane highway that wound through rather desolate countryside. Philip revved the engine and then started off, eager to begin the three-hour trip before the snow became worse.

Twenty miles outside the small town, the snow flurries turned into a thick blanket of large flakes that splatted against the windshield of the car. The black road had become light gray, barely distinguishable from the empty fields alongside it. The idea of turning back occurred to Philip; but the thought of the Like-Home Hotel, with its familiar security, beckoned him on. He'd driven in snow before, after all.

The blizzard blotted out the sun, and twilight fell over the landscape with a startling suddenness. Philip flicked on the headlights, only to find that they reflected back the fuzzy whiteness all around him. It was dark now. He was navigating the road by instinct, sensing when his tires slipped off the concrete and onto the rougher shoulder. Beads of sweat stood out on his forehead; Philip fought off the worries that crowded into his mind. What might happen next?

Then, almost like a miracle, a sign came into view. It was made of red neon letters that shone through the blizzard: RIGHT INN. At first Philip thought it was a direction sign: "right in." Then he grasped that there were two *n*'s in the last word. An inn, a motel, just when he desperately needed one. A red neon arrow pointed to the right. Philip braked and skidded for several feet. Then he turned to the right between two rows of thickly planted evergreens, his only clue to where the driveway might be. His tires spun as they climbed the steep incline. Finally Philip made it to the top. Ahead, he could see a large, gray-stone building. He parked the car, pulled his overnight case from the backseat, and locked the doors.

The Right Inn was a strange building. Even through the snowstorm, Philip could see that it wouldn't offer the predictable security that a Like-Home Hotel did. It didn't seem like a hotel at all, as a matter of fact. It looked like an old, deserted mansion.

In any other weather Philip would have gotten back into his car, turned around, and drove however many miles it was necessary to find a different motel. But this evening he had no choice. He walked up to the heavy wooden front door, grasped the carved iron handle, and pushed it open.

Philip walked inside, squinting his eyes to see in the dark, gloomy lobby. The heavy door slammed ominously behind him. There were no electric lights in the large room, just candles glowing from sconces on the walls and a huge, hanging candelabrum. Heavy drapes hung over the tall windows, and a fire leapt and crackled in the old fireplace.

Philip investigated the lobby more closely once his eyes had adjusted to the dim light. Was it possible that he had made a terrible mistake and walked into a private home? Perhaps the Right Inn was farther up the road somewhere, and he had stopped too soon. Just when Philip was ready to turn around and run back to his car, he noticed a small brass bell sitting on a long table in front of a red velvet curtain. Beside the bell was a large book with the word GUESTS embossed on it.

Philip noticed how badly his hands were trembling when he picked up the brass bell and gave it a sharp ring. Nothing happened. He rang the bell again. Then, from the interior of the inn, he heard footsteps approaching in his direction. They were heavy footsteps, quickening their pace as they came nearer.

The red velvet curtain suddenly parted in the middle and shot open. A man with black hair and a pale complexion stood before Philip, staring at him with inquisitive eyes.

"Yes?" he asked.

"I . . . I hoped you might have a room for the night," Philip said.

"We have every room in the house," the man said with a flourish of his right hand.

"With the weather like this, every other guest has canceled. You'll be all alone here. I've even had to let some of the staff go. Service may not be quite up to par, but we'll make your stay as interesting as possible. We don't like to disappoint a guest."

He finished his speech with a weird, forced smile that made Philip uneasy.

"Thank you," Philip said nervously, signing the guest book with the pen the man handed him. The ink was a strange, dark red color, rather like dried blood.

"You'll want dinner, I assume," the man said, running the fingers of one hand through his black hair, which grew in an odd widow's peak at the middle front of his forehead.

"Yes, certainly," Philip said, wondering if he would be able to order his usual pot roast and sauerkraut in a place like this.

"Very good, sir," the man said. "Dinner is served at seven o'clock in the dining room, off to the left. I'll show you to your room now. Since you're our only guest tonight, of course I'll give you the most sought-after room, number thirteen."

"Of course," Philip mumbled, feeling more like a prisoner than a guest as the man led him up a creaking staircase, down a shadowy hallway, and up to a door that had the number thirteen painted on it in red letters. The man handed Philip an old-fashioned brass key, excused himself, and hurried away.

Philip fit the key into the lock and opened the door. The room was pitch-black. He searched in his pockets for a pack of matches, found them, and struck a light. The glow from the match fell on a large candelabrum with five candles. Philip lit them and then looked around the room. An old four-poster bed with a canopy and heavy drapes falling from it dominated the room. He searched for a light switch, but there didn't seem to be any. Oddly enough, a television sat on a table at the end of the bed.

Philip tried to control his imagination as he unpacked his suitcase. Everything about the Right Inn seemed wrong; every aspect of it was totally unpredictable. He washed up, changed clothes, and went down to the dining room for dinner. He would have preferred to stay in his room, but he was starving.

The same man — he introduced himself as Mortimer — greeted Philip in the dining room. Mortimer explained that the inn had no menu. A standard meal was served to each guest, just the sort of food they would expect in such a place. While Philip waited to be served, he wondered what he was to expect.

The first course was a soup of a rather disturbing shade of red. There were odd, unidentifiable chunks in it. Despite his hunger, Philip pushed the bowl away from him, hoping it would be removed as soon as possible.

Mortimer delivered the main course on a silver platter covered by a silver dome. He set it on the table in front of Philip, then whisked off the lid. Philip stared down at the gray mass with finely convoluted ridges on its surface.

"Brain," Mortimer announced with his weird smile.

Philip looked away from the brain casserole and tried to regain control of his stomach. He stared at the stuffed animal heads mounted on the walls of the dining room. Their beady eyes all seemed to be watching him.

Mortimer took away the uneaten brain and the full bowl of soup. He assured Philip that he would find the next course delightful. It was a plate of peeled grapes and old, moldy cheese. Philip's hunger overcame his better judgment. He tried both a grape and a piece of cheese. Instantly he regretted it.

Mortimer appeared again and asked Philip if he would like to sample the dessert trolley.

"I'm going up to my room," Philip announced briskly, jumping up from the table. "I've had quite enough."

"Be sure to watch our special video," Mortimer called after him. "It's already in your VCR. You'll want to experience everything the inn has to offer."

Philip didn't turn around to answer. He ran up the stairs two at a time, opened the door to his room, then locked it tightly behind him. The candles still flickered, but they had burned down to short stubs. Philip looked at the television at the foot of the bed. What else was there to do? He would have to try the video.

He brushed his teeth, put on his pajamas, and crawled under the heavy covers of the bed. Then he flicked on the television and pushed the play button on the VCR.

There were several minutes of fuzziness until a picture came on the screen. Then Philip sat upright in bed. It was him! The picture was of him approaching the inn that night. The candlelight flickering on his face gave him a haunted look. What was going on here?

Philip watched himself on the screen, looking around the lobby, ringing the bell, and waiting for someone to appear. When Mortimer came out through the velvet curtain, the video suddenly moved on to a new scene. The camera followed a man's back as he walked through the rooms of the inn. Philip recognized the dining room. But his mouth went dry and his heart began to pound as the man descended a set of stairs into what at first seemed a cellar but turned out to be a dungeon. There were instruments of torture there, and heavy chains hanging on the walls.

The mysterious man whose face remained hidden from the camera walked from the dungeon up to a library on the first floor. The camera moved to the windows where horrible faces peered into the room. Philip clutched the covers around him. He watched in terror as the man moved from the library and up the staircase to the second floor. With a horrible inevitability, the man walked down the hallway and stopped in front of room thirteen. He knocked on the door.

Like an echo, there was a real knock on Philip's door. In the video the man knocked on the door again. Then the real knock came again. Philip was beginning to have trouble breathing. He looked at his door. Then he looked at the screen. The camera suddenly moved around to the man's face as he stood in front of room thirteen. It was a vampire, his fangs bared, his gleaming eyes staring straight at Philip!

A long, bloodcurdling shriek rose out of Philip's body. The knocking on his door grew louder and louder. Then a key rattled in the lock. Philip took one last look at the vampire's face on the screen before he fell into a dead faint.

Mortimer opened the door and rushed inside. He carried the candelabrum over to the nightstand and saw Philip's white face set in a look of terror. He turned to look at the television just as the credits to the movie flashed on the screen.

A feature presentation of
FRIGHT INN
The Fantasy Theme Hotel
for Horror Lovers

Mortimer bent down over Philip's limp body and felt his weak pulse. He rushed downstairs to the lobby and called the nearest hospital. He explained that one of the hotel guests had fainted while watching the Fright Inn video. The doctor told him to get the patient to the emergency room immediately.

Philip never stirred as Mortimer carried him out into the hotel van and put him in the backseat. Mortimer carefully maneuvered his van down the steep lane and out onto the main road. As he passed the hotel's sign he noticed that its first neon letter was not working.

Strange, he thought, that made it read: RIGHT INN.

The Collector

Toby sat on the porch alone in the middle of the night. His mother and father were asleep upstairs. He had come back outside because he couldn't sleep. It was the weird noises of the swamp creatures that disturbed him — the frogs and toads and insects and strange birds. He had lived in this place for a year now; still, its sounds were like a waking nightmare for him.

Toby reached for the box of matches his mother kept on the porch. He struck one against the rough, wooden boards of the floor. A flame flared up. With his free hand Toby lifted off the glass cover of the lantern, then touched the wick with the burning match. Fire. Toby set back the glass and stared at the flickering, dancing flame.

Now the fire was between him and the swamp beyond. The night sounds no longer frightened him. Toby felt that he was master of the swamp and its creatures ... especially the moths. They would soon be drawn to the fire, helplessly seeking its light.

The small moths came first. They circled the lantern, dizzying themselves to be near the light. They landed on the glass, then flew off, driven away by the heat. Yet they were always drawn back to the hypnotic light.

The first large moth appeared. Toby examined it carefully. He had caught one like it the previous week; it was mounted upstairs. Already Toby had an extensive collection of moths. They had become his passion.

More moths appeared, exotic ones with finely detailed markings. Toby reached behind him for the net and raised it up, ready to swoop down on his prey. A rare moth floated into the light on its orange-and-brown wings. It circled the lantern, confused. Toby held his breath. He had seen a picture of it only once, at the house of the old woman who lived down the road. She had told him a superstitious story about this rare moth. The old collectors in the area said that other moths would seek revenge on anyone who killed it.

Toby raised the net high in the air. The moth circled the lantern again. With a clean swoop he trapped it in his net. He could hear its strong wings beating against the mesh. He could sense its desire to live and be free. Toby set the net on the porch floor and ran noiselessly upstairs to his room to get a killing jar.

He flicked on his desk light and chose the largest jar he had. Carefully he squeezed a few drops of poisonous fluid into the bottom of the jar. He turned off the light and carried the jar down the stairs, his heart pounding.

As Toby opened the screen door, he sensed a difference in the air. More moths were circling the lantern in a frenzy. The trapped moth was throwing its thick body against the net and then falling to the floor in desperate attempts to escape. Toby set the killing jar on the floor and opened the lid. With a swift movement he picked up the net and shook the moth into the jar. It fluttered wildly against the glass. Then Toby fastened the lid on tight. He watched his victim struggle against the deadly fumes.

Suddenly he felt a strange weight on his neck. He whirled around in disgust and brushed away the huge moth that had landed on his body. Looking around, Toby saw that the air was thick with them. He sprang up from the killing jar and ran t the screen door, flailing his arms to ward off the moths that were suddenly closing in around him like a suffocating blanket.

Safely inside the house, Toby locked the screen door behind him. He looked back onto the porch and saw silhouettes of moths pressing their bodies against the screen. He could hear their wings beating. Toby shut the wooden door and double-locked it. He would have to leave the lantern and killing jar on the porch all night. Shuddering, he went up to his room.

Toby didn't turn on the light but crept into bed and pulled a sheet over his body. He imagined that the moths were outside searching for him, trying to find his room.

The old woman's story haunted his troubled thoughts. She said its markings were like an evil eye, casting bad luck on whoever captured it. She told him about a man who had once caught the moth and put it in his collection. Soon afterward he disappeared and was never seen again.

Toby was sweating under the sheet. He thought about running onto the porch and opening the killing jar. The moth could still be alive. But the thought of the thick, furry body on his neck and the hundreds of wings flapping around his face held him back. Like the moth, he would have to lie still and slowly, slowly, go to sleep.

Toby woke the next morning to the sound of his mother's voice. She called out to tell him that she was going into town. Toby looked at the clock and saw that it was nine o'clock. He didn't have school. His father had already left for work. Toby would be alone in the house.

Suddenly he remembered the moth and the disturbing dreams that had awakened him over and over during the night. Dressing quickly, he hurried downstairs. The killing jar sat on the kitchen table. The huge moth lay dead at the bottom, its beautiful wings limp against the glass.

Toby wanted to take the jar outside and throw it into the deepest part of the swamp. But he knew it was too late. The moth was dead; he might as well mount it.

Toby had no appetite for breakfast. He took the killing jar upstairs to his room and set it on a worktable next to the spreading board he used to dry his specimens. Using a forceps, he pulled the moth out of the jar and set its thick body into the groove of the board. He pushed a pin through the moth's thorax, feeling a wave of nausea and fear come over him. Quickly he set the wings at right angles to the body and fastened them down with pins and paper strips. It was done.

The old woman's superstition crowded back into his mind and wouldn't go away. Toby decided to take the moth to her house and show it to her. Perhaps she had been talking about another species, perhaps he was worrying needlessly. . . .

Toby came out of the path that ran along the swamp between the two houses. Carefully holding the spreading board in front of him, he climbed the steps to her porch and knocked on the door.

The old woman stared at him through her screen door. Her eyes dropped down to the moth on the board. Toby looked down at it, too. The lower orange wings each had a conspicuous eye spot that seemed to stare back at him. He looked up and met the woman's gaze. Her eyes were filled with terror.

"Take it away from here," she said in a quivering voice. "I warned you."

Toby hesitated on the porch. He wanted her to ease his fear. But instead, she was stirring panic inside him.

"Take it away," the woman screamed. "You have done the harm. I want no part of it!"

Toby gripped the board and ran away along the path by the edge of the swamp, back to his house. The spots on the moth's wings stared up at him like omens of evil.

Toby went about his chores the rest of the day, avoiding sight of the moth. He picked at his food at the dinner table, unable to eat. He sat in front of the television all evening, not knowing what he heard or saw.

It was finally time for bed. Toby reluctantly went to his room when his parents turned off the downstairs lights. He took one quick glance at the moth lying dead on the spreading board. Then he switched off his lamp and slipped under the covers of the bed, hiding in the shadowy night.

The sounds of the swamp crept into his room, the sounds of frogs and toads and insects and strange birds. He tried to block out the noises, but they grew louder and louder.

There was a strange thud against his screen. Toby sat up in bed and looked at the window with the moonlight streaming through it. He saw the silhouette of two large wings and a long, thick body pressed against the screen . . . a moth. Toby held his breath and waited. There was another thud, then another. He looked at the window and watched the moonlight being blotted out by more and more moths. Finally he sat in total darkness.

The air was heavy. Toby's breath came in short gasps. Then he heard the first delicate ripping of the screen. A louder sound, the sound of metal being torn at viciously, followed. The air was suddenly filled with beating wings. Toby could hear them coming toward him. He jumped from the bed and ran for the door and down the steps. He wanted to scream, but the moths were too close to his mouth. They were everywhere, flying around him.

He ran for the porch door and out into the night. For a minute he felt a rush of fresh air fill his lungs. Then the moths surrounded him again — more of them, huge ones and tiny ones. They pursued him across the yard and into the swamp. They drove him through pools of water filled with snakes and thick weeds, and across fallen, rotting trees. They chased him into the deepest, darkest part of the swamp.

No one ever saw Toby again. It was as though he had disappeared from the earth without a trace. The only clue he left was the torn screen, mysteriously ripped to shreds. They sent out search parties into the swamp. But no search party ever went where Toby had gone.

No one could have ever found that deep, dark place in the swamp where the moths had put Toby, pinned against a tree, in their human collection.

A Ghost Story

It was a dark, stormy night in late October,
the night before Halloween. Jagged streaks
of lightning shot across the sky, illuminat-
ing the old house that stood alone on top of
the hill. The wind howled through the tall
oaks that surrounded the house. Falling
leaves and heavy raindrops splatted
against the paned windows.

Inside, in a room lit by the flames of a
roaring fireplace and a single lamp, Dana
sat alone on the couch. She shivered and
drew the blanket she was wrapped in closer
to her neck. But it wasn't the cold wind or
the jagged lightning that had made her
shiver. It was the book of ghost stories she
was reading.

The story she was reading now had made
her blood run cold. It was about a ghost
that haunted an old graveyard. One cold
night the ghost let out a mournful moan.
He missed the house where he had once
lived. The ghost went to the nearby town

and searched frantically for his home. He went from house to house, knocking on the doors. But no door opened for him. Until, finally, he saw an old house sitting on a hill. The ghost began his weary climb up to the house. . . .

Dana stopped reading. She put the book down on her lap and searched the dark corners of the room with her eyes. Had she really heard something? Or was it just her imagination getting carried away? She sat very still for several moments. All she could hear was the cold wind howling around the house and through the trees.

Dana picked up the book and began to read again. But before she could get back into the story, she heard a loud rapping sound . . . a rapping on the front door of the house. Dana sat very still. She waited, wondering if the rapping would go away. But it didn't. It came again, louder than before. Whoever was there was not going away.

Dana pushed off the blanket and got up from the couch. She hesitated in front of the fireplace, staring into its leaping flames. Should she see who was at the door? It was probably a neighbor. Or maybe it was someone from her class. But maybe, her mind whispered, it was. . . .

Dana fought off the crazy idea that had

just come to her. She walked out of the living room and into the hallway. Without hesitating, she pulled open the door.

"Hi," a timid voice said out of the dark.

Dana's face dropped with disappointment. It was the new boy in her class. He had a pad and pencil in his hand, and he was dripping with water.

"I was just wondering," he said, "if your family might like to subscribe to some magazines. I'm selling them for the stamp club."

"Come on in," Dana said. She opened the door wider for the boy to walk inside the hallway.

"You're Jason, right?" she said.

Jason nodded his head. "Would you like to buy a magazine?" he asked eagerly.

"No, not exactly," Dana answered, leading him into the room where she had been reading. "It's just that I don't want to be alone right now."

"What do you mean?" Jason asked, looking around the dimly lit room with its heavy curtains and strange antiques standing in corners.

"What I mean," Dana said, "is that I don't want to be alone because I'm afraid."

"Afraid of what?"

"Of ghosts," Dana said in a low voice, almost like a whisper.

Jason's eyes darted around the room again. Even though he was new in town, he had already heard weird things about this house. It was one of the oldest in the area. Some of the boys in his class had warned him not to come here to try to sell magazines. They had told him to forget it. Now he wished he had.

"You're not afraid of ghosts, are you?" Dana asked, her voice trembling slightly.

"Ah . . . no," he answered.

Just then a piece of wood made a loud crack in the fireplace. Jason jumped. A minute later there was a strange scraping sound over their heads. Jason followed Dana's wide eyes up to the ceiling. The sound dragged across the floor above them again. Jason stared at Dana, his eyes taking on a frightened gleam.

"What was that?"

Dana sunk back into the warmth of the overstuffed couch and pulled the blanket up around her.

"It always starts that way," she murmured.

"I don't know what you're talking about," Jason said, getting up from his chair. "But I think it's time for me to go."

Dana reached out an arm and pulled on Jason's coat sleeve.

"No. Don't leave me alone tonight.

Please. I just can't face it by myself!"

Jason looked down at Dana's pleading face. He wavered for a minute; then slowly he sat back down.

"It's true what they say about this house," Dana whispered as though some other ears were listening and trying to hear what she had to say. "It really is haunted."

She suddenly stopped as a tapping sound began over their heads. *Tap. Tap-tap. Tap-tap-tap.* The sound moved across the ceiling from one side of the room to another.

"What is that?" Jason asked, trying to sound brave.

"A sword," Dana said. "The ghost is a dead soldier who was killed in the Civil War. He lived here before he went off to join the Union Army."

A cold sweat was standing out on Jason's forehead now. He wondered if Dana was unbalanced; she sat there on the couch like a statue, not moving. He wanted to run out the door and never come back. He started to get up out of his chair again.

"Wait," Dana cried out. "I can hear it in the hallway."

Jason strained his ears to hear. There it was. The tapping had started at the top of the high, winding staircase. He suddenly felt as though all the strength had drained out of his legs. He looked over at Dana, who was staring back at him in stark terror.

"It's never come this close before," she whispered. "Before, it always stayed upstairs."

The sound grew louder and louder each moment. The sword scraped against the steps. The tapping noise followed it. Jason inched away from the couch where Dana sat as still as death. He moved toward the door to the hallway. If only he knew another way to escape. But he had to pass the staircase. Finally he couldn't stand it any longer. He dashed out into the hallway.

"It's him!" Dana screamed.

Jason's legs were rooted to the floor in terror. He looked up the long, winding staircase. Coming down was a figure in a blue Civil War uniform. He held a cane in his hand and wore a sword at his side.

Jason let out a bloodcurdling scream and ran for the door. He gave one terrified, backward glance before stumbling out into the stormy night.

The soldier began to run down the steps after him. He stopped when he saw Dana rush into the hallway.

"Who was that?" he demanded.

Dana gave her father an innocent smile.

"A new boy in my class," she said. "He thought you were a ghost."

"Poor kid," Dana's father said. "Why didn't you tell him I'm going to a Halloween party?"

But Dana didn't answer. She was already back on the couch, reading her favorite ghost story for the twentieth time.

In the Lantern's Light

The hoot of the train whistle slowly died away in the cool night air. Ben sat upright and tense in the empty boxcar, listening to the screech of the wheels on the tracks as the train braked and finally stopped.

For minutes he didn't flinch a muscle. Why had the train stopped? Would they come looking in the boxcar and find him?

It was the first time Ben had hopped a train. He had done it, almost without thinking, as he walked along the rail yards of his hometown. He was still young, and life seemed to be moving too slow.

The train gave a sudden, short jerk, then stopped again. Ben was thrown forward on his face. He picked himself up and walked over to the big sliding door of the boxcar. Cautiously he pushed it open.

Open countryside, lit by the moon, stretched away for miles in all directions. Ben figured he was in Nebraska by now. The train had been moving for nearly ten hours since he'd jumped aboard. But why had it stopped out here in this desolate place?

He stuck his head out farther and looked up and down the long line of boxcars. The engine stood silent at the front of the train, its nose nudging the edge of night.

Then Ben caught sight of a lantern light, swinging and winking its way along the side of the train. As it drew nearer he made out the dark, shadowy figure of the man who carried it. The man stopped at a boxcar that was eight up from his. Ben heard its door slide open roughly. He saw the man lift his lantern and peer inside.

Ben felt a sudden impulse to run into the farthest corner of the boxcar and hide. But he knew the lantern's light could still find him there. He watched as the man walked along the tracks to the next boxcar and searched it. Who could he be looking for?

Ben knew he had to act fast. Carefully and quietly he pushed open the door of the boxcar until it was wide enough for his body to fit through. Then, taking a deep gulp of air, he jumped out into the mysterious night.

He fell through the darkness for what seemed an eternity. Then he hit the rough gravel of the rail embankment with a thud.

Still stunned, he rolled his body down the bank and into the dark.

The lantern light swung over to where he had landed. The man had heard him. Ben pulled himself into the shadows of a clump of bushes. The lantern swayed across where he hid. The light struck his eyes and, for a second, blinded him. There was a grunt from the man. Then Ben heard him slam shut the door of the boxcar.

Long minutes passed. Ben crouched in the bushes, afraid to move. Finally the man with the lantern seemed satisfied. He swung his light back up to the front of the train.

Ben moved out of his hiding place. He started to climb back up the embankment toward the boxcar. Halfway up, he slid down in the loose gravel. As he started up again, the train suddenly jerked forward. Then, slowly, the wheels of the cars began to turn. Ben dug his feet into the gravel and scrambled up to the rails. The train was picking up speed. He lunged for the boxcar door and tried to open it. It wouldn't budge. He ran alongside it, tugging on the door. Then, suddenly, the train was going too fast. Ben let go of the boxcar and fell away from the cars and onto the hard gravel. He covered his face with an arm to keep the dust spun up by the wheels out of his eyes. When he finally dropped his arm, the caboose of the train was drawing away into the night.

Ben stared after the train until it disappeared from sight. He could hear its sounds on the tracks for several minutes more. Then he was left alone under the endless sky, dotted with brilliant stars. He gazed up at them, feeling more alone than he had ever felt in his life. The call of a night bird sent a chill through his body. He looked at the empty, desolate country around him. There was no place to find shelter, no place to feel safe.

Ben felt that the stars were watching him like eyes in the night. He stood up and stepped onto the wooden ties that supported the rails. He began to walk, heading back in the direction from which the train had come. He remembered that a half hour earlier it had passed through a small town, blowing its warning whistle as it went through a crossing. It would take him several hours to get there on foot, but he couldn't stay in this barren place alone.

He stretched his stride out to match the space between the ties. For an hour he walked steadily on, staring down at his feet as he set one down after another on the ties. Suddenly Ben sensed a strangeness in the air and looked up.

A hundred yards in front of him, on the right side of the embankment, a bonfire was burning. Its flames jumped up into the sky, casting an eerie glow around it.

Ben's heart pounded faster. Who else might be out here in the middle of nowhere . . . at night? He wanted to hide, but there were no trees, no hills. He crouched down close to the rails and crept nearer. A figure suddenly stood up in front of the fire and poked it with a stick. It looked like an old man stooped with age. Ben decided he must be a hobo, an old traveler of the rails. The figure sat down again, next to a lantern on the ground.

Ben drew closer. Through the quiet night he began to hear a low, moaning sound. It grew louder as he approached the bonfire. The man's back was turned to Ben, and he rocked from side to side as he moaned.

Ben felt curious but not afraid. He walked down the embankment toward the bonfire. He knew the man must have heard his footsteps, but he still didn't turn around. Ben stopped and spoke.

"What is wrong?"

The moaning stopped, but there was no answer.

Ben stepped forward and lightly touched the shoulder of the man's jacket.

"Can I help you?" he asked.

The man shook his head back and forth. Ben stood still behind him, wondering what to do. Then he watched the man reach over and pick up the lantern by his side. Slowly he turned around to Ben, holding the lantern up to his face.

The face was empty; it was as smooth and blank as the surface of an egg.

Ben backed away, a scream choking in his throat. The man didn't move but kept his horrid, blank face turned toward Ben.

Ben scrambled back up the embankment. The man's smooth white face shone like the moon in the lantern's light. Ben ran from it in terror. The face haunted him mile after mile as he fled toward the town.

The night was still black when Ben finally saw the scattered lights of the town ahead of him. He finally found the courage to turn around and look behind him for the first time. No stooped figure with a blank face was following. Ben tried to tell himself that it had been a dream, a waking nightmare.

The lights of the town grew nearer. Ahead, Ben saw a station building on the left side of the tracks. A light was shining through its doorway. He hurried toward its comforting safety. Ben pushed open the door and walked inside. A white-haired man stood behind the ticket counter, working by the light of a lantern. The man raised his blue eyes to Ben.

"Good evening," he said in surprise when he saw Ben. "You look as pale as a sheet. Have you seen a ghost?"

"No, not a ghost," Ben said, his breath still coming in short gasps. "It was much worse."

The man stared at him with curiosity. "What do you mean?"

"It was an old man," Ben said. "But his face . . . it was horrible . . . it was — "

The man held up a hand to silence Ben. He slowly turned around and picked up the lantern from behind him.

"Was it . . . like this?"

He turned his face around to Ben. It was empty . . . as smooth and blank as the surface of an egg.

Then the light of the lantern went out.

Footsteps

Laurie hesitated before stepping out into the dark yard of the old house. The black skeletons of bare-limbed trees loomed against the charcoal sky. A cold November wind blew dead leaves in circles at her feet. Laurie found an old-fashioned wicker bench and sat down, facing her new home. Everything fell silent, eerily quiet.

Her family had moved into the house that day. It was a large, rambling Victorian, set on a hill several miles away from the town she had been living in. Laurie's friends had told her strange stories about the house. It had sat vacant for years before her parents had bought it one day on an impulse.

The old wicker bench creaked as Laurie turned around to look behind her. Nothing was there. She knew she should go inside to bed. But something was holding her back from facing the bedroom where her furniture and belongings had been put.

Her mother had insisted that the room was charming. But Laurie had felt uneasy in it. A heaviness had hung in the air, a strange gloom that was suffocating.

"Laurie," her father called from the doorway. "Are you out there?"

Laurie got up from the bench and walked toward the door. Her parents didn't understand how she felt. They didn't know the dread the house stirred in her.

"Time for bed," her father said when she walked into the hallway. "I hope we don't keep you awake. There's lots of unpacking we have to do yet tonight."

"Good night, Laurie," her mother said absentmindedly as she worked over a packing crate. "Sleep tight."

Laurie started up the wide staircase to the second floor. She wished she didn't have to go up by herself. But her parents had gone back to their work, forgetting about her.

Laurie walked into the large bedroom with its three windows and high ceilings. Her old furniture seemed lost in the room; she felt lost, too. She quickly put on her nightgown and then went out into the hall to the bathroom. On her way back she passed the door that went up to the third-floor attic. It was slightly ajar. The sight made her heart pound faster. She had just passed it a few minutes ago. She was sure it hadn't been open then. With trembling hands Laurie grasped the old doorknob and pushed it tightly shut. Then she hurried into her room and closed the door behind her.

She tossed and turned for almost an hour. Finally her parents came up the staircase to go to bed. They peeked in the room to check on her, but Laurie pretended to be asleep. She couldn't tell them she was frightened. She didn't want to admit it to herself.

The house became even more silent. She lay in the bed staring out her windows at the moonlit branches. Still, sleep would not come. Suddenly a sound made her nerves jump. It was a dull, scraping noise over her head. Laurie looked up toward the ceiling. She saw nothing but the murky shadows of night.

It came again . . . a sound of rough scuffing across the wood floor of the attic above. Laurie shrank back into her covers. She tried to think of all the things it might be. A squirrel inside the house. Something being blown by the breeze through a window left accidentally open. Then there was another sound. A more steady and deliberate sound. The sound of footsteps.

Laurie closed her eyes and shook her

head to clear it. She opened her eyes again. It wasn't a dream. She was wide-awake. And the sound was still there. The footsteps echoed down through the ceiling and filled the room. Laurie felt fear creep into her body and paralyze her. She lay in bed wondering if she was going mad. But the footsteps were too real. They had crossed to one side of the ceiling now.

Laurie suddenly heard a difference in them. The footsteps were moving down, down the stairway from the attic. She screamed out with all the terror trapped in her body.

Her parents stayed with Laurie until she finally fell into an exhausted sleep. They assured her it was a nightmare caused by anxiety about moving into the new house. Laurie didn't believe them. She knew she had heard the footsteps.

The next day there was no school. Laurie went through the motions of helping her parents settle into the house. In late afternoon her father asked her to go up into the attic with him. Laurie followed him up the stairs, a lump growing in her throat.

The attic was still crowded with the belongings of the elderly couple who had lived and died in the house. Boxes and old trunks were piled under layers of dust. Broken furniture huddled in the eaves. Laurie had seen the attic before, but she had never walked around in it. Her father pulled away a large trunk that blocked one of the small windows at the end of the room. When he was finished, Laurie walked over to look out at the view.

She stumbled over something on the floor. Looking down, she saw that it was a pair of men's shoes, worn and dirty. The brown leather was cracked and torn in several places. The shoes had taken on the shape of the feet that had once worn them. Laurie shrank back from them.

Then she ran past her father, down the stairs from the attic, and into her room. She fell onto her bed and buried her head in the pillow. Her father came in to ask what was the matter. Laurie couldn't tell him how she'd felt when she'd seen the shoes. He would think she was mad.

That night her parents tucked Laurie into bed and kissed her good night. She pretended to be calm and unafraid. But when they shut the door, strange thoughts flooded into her mind. They tortured her until she finally fell asleep on her tear-soaked pillow.

She awoke with a start, confused for a minute about where she was. She remembered . . . her new room, the new house.

Then she heard the sound that had awakened her, the sound of footsteps. They were
moving across the ceiling above her. The
footfalls were heavy and deliberate. The
steps reached the head of the attic staircase. Laurie opened her mouth to scream,
but nothing came out. She lay still, listening with terror as the footsteps moved
down, one at a time, toward her. Now she
heard them in the hallway outside. This
time her scream echoed through the house.

Her parents still didn't believe her. They
calmed her with assurances that it was all
a nightmare. They promised to take her to
a doctor as soon as they could get an ap-
pointment. Laurie finally fell asleep,
clutching her father's hand.

Again, the next day, her father forced
her to go with him up to the attic. He tried
to convince her that no ghosts or strange
spirits could be there. He held her arm as
she climbed the stairs. When they reached
the top, Laurie walked toward the window.
Her eyes settled on the spot where she had
seen the pair of shoes the day before. They
were gone.

"Where are they?" she asked her father.

He looked at her in confusion. Laurie
drew back, toward the stairs. Her feet
stumbled over something. Looking down,

she saw the pair of shoes. They were sitting nearer the staircase.

Her father promised she wouldn't have to go back up to the attic again. He would take her to see a doctor soon, a doctor who knew how to help her. Laurie nodded at everything he said. But she knew the footsteps would come to find her again.

Her parents took turns sitting with her that night. Her father was still there by her bedside when she fell asleep. When she awoke, she felt like a swimmer struggling up out of nightmares that were drowning her. She gasped for air and opened her eyes. The chair beside her bed was empty. She was all alone. And the footsteps had already reached the stairs.

They moved with an eerie, steady pace, always coming toward her, always growing louder. Laurie heard them stop at the bottom of the staircase. She held her breath for so long that she grew dizzy. Then the footsteps started down the hallway toward her room. She'd known they would.

There was no moon that night. The room was draped in a darkness so black that Laurie could not see the windows or the door. She could only wait for the sound of one footfall after another, coming closer and closer.

The door did not make a sound. But suddenly Laurie knew the footsteps were in her room. They fell, heavy and determined, against the bare floorboards. Fear choked back the scream welling up inside her. Now the footsteps were at the end of the bed. In only a few minutes they would be. . . .

Laurie's scream echoed in her mind like a dream. Before it ended, her father and mother were in the room. They flicked on the light and ran to her.

The footsteps had stopped. Laurie stared wildly at her father as he rushed to her and then stumbled over something on the floor. Together they looked down.

There, next to her bed, sat the pair of brown, worn shoes.

A Night in the Woods

The five boys gathered at the school parking lot in late afternoon. They carried neatly rolled sleeping bags and carefully packed knapsacks. They were waiting for their leader, Mr. Robinson, to take them on a camping trip. There was an edge of nervous anticipation in the air.

"Wonder where old Robbie is," Ty said. "He's never late like this."

"Probably getting more food," Paul answered. "Remember how much we ate last trip?"

The boys sighted a black van driving down the road toward them. Mr. Robinson pulled into the parking lot with a broad smile on his face.

"Got some extra food," he called out as he jumped from the van.

The boys broke into clapping and cheering. They had been camping with Mr. Robinson for three years now. He was like a father to them.

"We've got a long way to drive," Mr. Robinson said. "I'm taking you to a place where we've never camped before. Let's get rolling."

The boys threw their gear into the back of the van and piled into the seats. Ty sat up front with Mr. Robinson. Paul and Nick shared the middle seat. Brad and Ron wedged into the backseat with the sleeping bags and knapsacks. Ty always tried to sit by Mr. Robinson. He was the youngest of the boys.

"Where we going, Robbie?" Brad yelled from the back.

"It's called Wolf Ridge," Mr. Robinson answered. "I went there a long time ago with another good group — like you guys."

"That's a state park, isn't it?" Paul asked. "I heard something creepy about it once."

"The state owns the land," Mr. Robinson said. "But not many people go there. It's too wild for the kind of camping amateurs like to do."

Ty turned around. "What did you hear about it that was creepy, Paul?"

"Just a story my older brother told me. Forget it."

A long silence filled the van. Ty and Nick saw the scared look on Paul's face. They turned away and stared out at the trees along the highway, wondering what he was thinking.

After two hours of driving, Mr. Robinson asked Brad and Ron to pass out the sandwiches he had packed in a cooler in the back. Once their stomachs were full, the boys began to joke around again. They almost forgot what Paul had said.

"How much longer till we get there, Robbie?" Brad asked. "It's going to be dark soon, isn't it?"

Mr. Robinson checked his watch.

"We'll be at the park station in half an hour."

"Why are we stopping at the station?" Paul asked.

"Wolf Ridge is a wild area. We need a ranger to take us into the park where we'll spend the night. I'm just not that familiar with it anymore."

"You sure this is a good idea, Robbie?" Ty whispered. "I mean, we could have camped closer to home."

"I heard that," Nick said. "Ty's afraid again, aren't you, Ty?"

The rest of the boys laughed, except Paul. He knew how Ty felt.

Twilight was dimming the sky as the van pulled into a rutted lane edged by towering pine trees.

"We're almost there," Mr. Robinson said. "The station is right ahead."

"Looks deserted," Nick said. "What kind of person would want to be a ranger here?"

"I think it looks creepy," Ty added.

Nobody made fun of him for sounding scared. This park was different from anyplace they had camped before. It seemed like the end of the world.

Mr. Robinson parked the van about two hundred yards from the station, which was set back from the entry road. He told the boys to unpack their gear while he went in and got the ranger. They watched him walk up to the station, push open the door, and disappear from sight. Then they got busy sorting out the sleeping bags, knapsacks, and supplies.

"Hurry up," Brad yelled at Ty. "Let's get loaded up so we can start walking in. I don't like getting a campsite ready this late."

"Look, there's the ranger," Nick said, pointing to a man in a brown uniform coming out of the station.

"Wonder where Robbie is," Ty added.

"Evening, boys," the ranger called out as he approached them. "I'm Harris. Mr. Robinson asked me to take you into the woods."

The boys stared at the ranger. He had a full beard and dark, beady eyes. He looked like he hadn't been in civilization for a long time.

"Where's Robbie?" Ty asked again.

"He's making some calls to your parents, to let them know where you are," the ranger said in a rough voice. "Now let's get moving. It's getting dark."

The boys fell in line behind Harris, trudging through the thick underbrush that was beginning to lose its color and form in the shadowy twilight.

"I don't like him," Ron whispered to Brad. "Did you see how hairy he is? Weird!"

Brad was turning something over and over in his mind.

"How could Robbie be making calls to our parents?" he whispered back. "I didn't see any telephone lines."

The two boys' eyes met in a troubled stare.

"Don't mention that to Ty," Ron said. "He'd freak out."

The ranger led them through the woods for an hour. Each boy tried to remember landmarks to guide him back by. But the darkness made it difficult for them to stay oriented. Finally Harris stopped in the middle of a clearing surrounded by tall pines.

"You'll camp here," he ordered. "Two of you find wood for the fire; the rest of you lay out the sleeping bags in a circle and unpack the supplies."

"How will Robbie find us?" Ty asked. "We can't camp without him."

"I'll go look for him," Harris said with a growl. "Maybe the old man got lost in the woods."

The ranger gave the boys a final, hard stare and then slipped away into the darkness.

"At least there's a full moon," Nick said. "Robbie will be able to see by that."

The boys went to work, mechanically doing the things Robbie had taught them to prepare for the night. Nobody spoke; each kept his fears to himself.

An eerie, drawn-out howl echoed through the forest. The boys dropped what they were doing and gathered in a tight circle around the fire site.

"Hurry up and light the fire," Brad said. "It'll keep away animals . . . or whatever might be out there."

Nick struck a safety match and quickly held it out to the pile of dried wood they had collected. The flames jumped up into the night and glowed on the drawn faces of the five boys.

"Think we should go back and check on Robbie?" Nick asked.

"How could we ever find him?" Ron said. "We'd just get lost ourselves."

"Paul, what did you hear about this place?" Ty suddenly asked in a trembling voice.

"It was just some dumb story," Paul said. "You don't want to hear it."

"What was it, Paul?" Brad demanded, grabbing Paul's arm tighter than he had planned to.

"A bunch of guys, like us, went camping at Wolf Ridge," Paul began. "I think it was about eight years ago. Nobody knows what happened to them. They just never came back. My brother told me a lot of weird stories about what might have happened. . . ."

Everyone fell silent and stared into the fire. Ty was clenching his teeth to keep from crying. Even Brad looked scared. Suddenly Harris appeared in front of them without having made a sound. They all jumped when they saw him.

"Where's Robbie?" Brad demanded.

"He must be lost in the woods," the

ranger said. "All of you will have to help me find him."

"Why didn't we wait for him in the first place?" Ron asked. "Then he wouldn't have gotten lost."

"He didn't have to call our parents," Brad added. "You don't have a telephone, anyway."

Harris stared down at Brad with a mean scowl on his face. Brad could see the red fire reflected in his dark eyes.

"Stand up!" the ranger ordered him. "You're coming out first."

Brad stood up reluctantly.

"Where's he going?" Nick asked the ranger in a frightened voice.

"To find Robbie," Harris said. "The rest of you stay here till I come back to get you."

Brad bent down and pretended to tie his shoe.

"Remember our whistle," he whispered to the others. "Every fifteen minutes. That way we'll keep track of each other."

Harris led Brad away from the warm circle of fire into the black shadows of the woods. Ron, Nick, Paul, and Ty edged closer together.

"What's going on?" Ty whispered.

"I don't know," Paul said.

"But he's the ranger," Nick added. "We've got to do what he says, especially since Robbie isn't here."

A short time later Harris came back. He signaled for Ron to follow him. They walked off into the woods in the opposite direction in which Brad had gone.

"Maybe we're fanning out, to form something like a net to find Robbie," Paul said.

He met the others' eyes and saw the fear shining in them.

"Brad should be whistling soon," Ty said quietly.

Harris reappeared in the circle of light. He looked over the three who were left. He pointed to Nick. Nick got to his feet, cast a backward glance at Ty and Paul, and followed the ranger into the shadows of the night.

A few minutes later Ty and Paul heard a strange sound. But it wasn't a whistle.

"I feel sick," Ty said.

"Maybe we should take off and run," Paul whispered.

The two boys searched the dark woods around them for an escape route.

"It's too late," Ty whispered back. "There he is again."

The ranger stood there, looking first at one boy and then the other. Finally he motioned to Paul. Paul slowly got up to his feet. He leaned over to put a hand on Ty's shoulder. Then Harris grabbed him by the arm and pulled him into the woods.

Ty sat alone by the campfire. He felt panic stirring in his stomach and then through his whole body. Suddenly he remembered the whistle. He pursed his lips and made the shrill sound that the boys used as their special call.

The whistle broke the unnatural stillness of the woods. It echoed among the towering pines. But then it died, and no one returned Ty's call.

Ty scrambled to his feet. He looked wildly in all directions, trying to decide which way to run. He turned around, and like a nightmare, Harris stood there staring at him.

The stillness of the woods was broken again. Ty's screams mixed in the night air with the eerie howl of the werewolf.